City of
Broad Shoulders

City of
Broad Shoulders

An Esmée Anderson Experience

No. 1

E. S. Holland

Maidenhead Hall • 2015

Published by Maidenhead Hall, an imprint of Twelve Winters Press.

P. O. Box 414 • Sherman, Illinois 62684-0414
maidenhead hall • twelvewinters.com

City of Broad Shoulders was first published by Maidenhead Hall in 2015.

Cover and interior page design by TWP Design.

Front cover photo copyright © 2006 John Peri. All rights reserved. Back cover photo © 2015 John Peri. All rights reserved. Visit photo.net/photos/johnperi.

ISBN
978-0-9861597-6-3

Printed in the United States of America

Acknowledgments

First, I would like to acknowledge my debt to my writers' group—*les femmes de Café de la Nouvelle Mairie*—for your friendship and unwavering encouragement, and for sharing the details of your *escapades*. Also, thank you to my friends at Columbia College in the heart of the City of Broad Shoulders for your invaluable assistance in finding a publisher for this little book. Finally, a special note of thanks to photographer John Peri.

for A.N. & H.M.

City of
Broad Shoulders

Stormy, husky, brawling,
City of Big Shoulders:

They tell me you are wicked and I
   believe them . . .

Carl Sandburg, "Chicago"

The flight from Paris to Chicago had left me jetlagged—that was true—but the argument I'd had with Christopher had taken something out of me too, so I was already feeling exhausted when I boarded at de Gaulle. As long as Christopher and I communicated only with our bodies, which sang together like perfectly tuned strings, the sex so perfect it seemed choreographed beforehand, our relationship worked. But eventually the time came for coffee and croissant and relating to each other as people, not simply insatiable sexual beings, and invariably things would fall apart.

Even as I reflected on the impossible nature of our relationship (for lack of a better word)—turning on the jets in the hotel room's marble and glass shower—I thought of Christopher's sculpted tummy, and felt my hands on his chiseled hips, then the tensed roundness of his ass. . . . By that point his beautifully veined cock would be defying gravity, though seemingly as heavy and as hard as a chunk of granite. . . .

I would miss fucking him to be sure. It'd been twelve hours. He was probably already screwing that slut Giselle who lived two floors down, jamming his rock-hard breakup anger into her tight dancer's ass. The pert little whore would taste her own shit while greedily sucking him off.

Before stepping into the shower I glanced at the mirror and thought that I'm tired of the red highlights—maybe I should mark my break with Christopher by going blond. The only person in the world I trusted with such an operation was Marcus, and I wouldn't be in L.A. for another month. Oh well, raven red it would be for a few more weeks. I was meeting the Kims here in two days and guiding them on a two-week experience in Singapore. (In exotic travel, we don't do "vacations" or "trips"; we do "experiences.") The Kims were both doctors—one an M.D., the other a Ph.D., but I couldn't recall which was which. The experience had something to do with either his or her work, at least in part. I'd have a long enough flight to hear all about it. Just about twenty-four hours, give or take.

I adjusted the shower jets to pulsate and stepped around the glass partition. The hot water kneading my body from multiple directions felt heavenly. I worked the hotel's exfoliating gel into my shoulders and neck, the small of my back, my butt, then my stomach and ribs, hips and thighs. My body felt taut even though I hadn't been on an elliptical or lifted a weight in nearly three weeks. Sex with Christopher was athletic and intense, leaving little energy and even less need to go to the gym. The hotel's fitness center was on the sixth floor, and I'd pay a visit to its machines tomorrow. Promise.

I'd brought my electric razor into the shower and used it to smooth my legs. Then I clipped the sharply Brazilian edges of my pubes. I couldn't help thinking of Christopher's kisses along my honeyed lips and the tip of his probing tongue as it briséd along the edges of my pleasure.

It was a mistake to recall it: my honey was beginning to flow. I didn't want to give Christopher the secret compliment of thinking of him while I got myself off. I wanted to hold onto my liberating anger. I would give my vibrator the cold shoulder for tonight (Lady's travel tip: The "Discreet Pete" will get past the TSA and even Customs every time). The exhaustion of jetlag would let me sleep. No question.

The sheets at the Renaissance were known for their silkiness. I didn't even bother with panties before slipping between them. I hadn't bothered with the blackout curtains either, so when I turned off the side lamp, the city lights angled throughout the room. I closed my eyes and waited for the utter exhaustion of international travel, combined with the unique exhaustion that accompanies a breakup, to flood over me like Maui's gentle surf. I willed myself to think of the red and orange poppies that grow along the lanes of Périgueux, to smell their potent fragrance, to hear the bees collecting their nectar in early summer.

I tried . . . but again and again I returned to the sensation of Christopher's cock filling my pussy, the salty taste of his balls and how one would roll past my lips like a kiwi—and the sound of the pleasure he purred as I sucked and rolled the kiwi with my tongue.

Fucking Christopher—why do you have to be such a douche when we're not fucking?

I lay in the comfortable bed trying to fall asleep. On the other side of the world it was time to wake up, and my clock-confused (and cock-obsessed) brain decided to be in sync with that hemisphere.

I turned on the lamp. It was going on midnight and I was wide awake. I wanted to read, but I didn't want to be taunted by the bed. Ruben's coffeehouse and bookstore was only a few blocks away—and open all night. I dressed in jeans and my favorite sweater, and did the barest of makeup. I'd loaded my Kindle a week before with new titles (enough for months of reading), but I'd also bought an old copy of Austen's *Pride and Prejudice* in a secondhand shop on rue de Rivoli. Its smell and feel appealed to me at the moment more than the sterility of my beloved Fire.

It was eight or so blocks to the bookshop—the night breeze was refreshing as it swirled between the buildings—and I found Ruben's just as I recalled it: a classic shop with a high tin ceiling, tall bookcases with a librarian's ladder on a track, overstuffed chairs and sofas here and there, glaringly mismatched other than in their quaintness.

I ordered a chai tea from the bar in the back of the store, then found a comfy leather chair to curl up in. I opened my book to the plight of Mr. and Mrs. Bennet and their five daughters. I first read *Pride and Prejudice* in high school and found it romantic, I suppose, but when I read it again after college—perhaps because I spent much of my senior year balling my British lit professor—I saw Netherfield Park and Pemberley as metaphors for Bingley's and Darcy's manhoods. After all, Lizzie reconsiders Mr. Darcy's prideful personality only after she discovers the size of his *estate*, and suddenly she appreciates his, well, stiffness. Jane will be adequately taken care of by Mr. Bingley's assets, but lucky Lizzie. . . .

The Ruben's barista brought my tea and sat it on a small table next to my chair. She was a redheaded wench with emerald, feline eyes— likely the reason so many men were camped out in the bookstore, nearly all managing a seat that afforded them a view of the bar and its comely maid. Except one patron, who sat near the entrance, facing the street. I think I noticed him mainly because he didn't seem to notice me. Gay maybe? Now I viewed him in profile. I liked the way his brown hair fell over his ear and the collar of an indigo denim shirt. He wore plastic-framed glasses, black, that were sliding just a bit down his subtly aquiline nose. I wondered about the color of his eyes—

Knock it off, weirdo. If you're interested in trawling, you should've painted on the little black dress and gone to a club. This is about drying out from your Christopher binge and being able to sleep . . . eventually.

I focused my attention on the impending Netherfield ball, when Mrs. Bennet hopes to snare Bingley to marry Jane and save them all from being turned out when Mr. Bennet dies in the unfortunate state of not having a male heir. It was all very pomp-and-circumstance, but in essence Mrs. Bennet was baiting Mr. Bingley with the promise of her eldest daughter's nicely ripe cunt, which had been as well guarded as the queen's crown. Jane was more than marrying age, and pussy had a pretty short shelf-life in Austen's England. The well-heeled gentlemen visiting from "town" (i.e. London) would no doubt stick their moneyed pricks in any servant girl's snatch, but they must save their heir-bearing fucks for brides with pristine pussies, hymens as intact as the trestles beneath London Bridge.

I sipped my tea. It was good.

"Ah, *Pride and Prejudice*. Which of the sisters do you most relate to?" It was the guy with glasses—he had a squarish jaw, lightly stubbled . . . and brown eyes. Before I could respond, he continued, "Let's see . . . the lovely but taciturn Jane, or outspoken and fiery Elizabeth? Surely not painfully buttoned-up Mary . . . ?"

"Don't forget, Mary is a musician—never sell short the brooding, artistic types."

"Then there's 'the most determined flirt' Lydia—awfully impulsive," he said. He held a thick book against his hip, but I couldn't make out its title. He was taller than I might've guessed, six-one, six-two maybe. The untucked denim shirt over brown jeans was loose-fitting but there was a broadness in his chest and shoulders, and I imagined a nicely sculpted tummy—but I may have been projecting Christopher's abs, the sight of which always turned me on.

"Impulsive, yes," I said, "but likely good company for a long weekend."

He smiled. Nice teeth. "What about Kitty? Just as fun but minus some crazy?"

"I wonder at your premise." The chair I was in was low, and I was eye-to-eye with where his belt buckle would be if he wore one beneath the shirt—I suspected he didn't: he seemed that casual. I had an impulse to lift his shirt enough to test my hunch, and while I was at it, the one about his abs too. Instead, "Can one be just as fun *minus* some crazy?"

He flashed those nice teeth again. "Excellent point. Enjoy your book." He continued to the bar, where he got a refill on his coffee, then returned to his place near the door. He smiled and those brown eyes made full contact as he went by. I smelled his fragrant dark roast . . . and admired his verso all the way back to his chair. O.k., he wasn't gay, not with those razor-sharp flirting skills. I was no amateur, and he had me back on my heels throughout the volley.

Back to the Bennet girls.

I found Austen's prose as musical as always, the chai was perfect drinking temperature, and the chair in Ruben's was perfectly cozy—yet I couldn't keep myself from glancing over at Mr. Brown Eyes every so often. He appeared engrossed in his thick book, which lay on the table before him; he was about two-thirds through the tome. During one of my recon glances he used a little yellow pencil—like one might use to keep score in miniature golf—to scribble a note in the book. So he was a professor or a writer or something like that. Not moneyed, then, like Misters Bingley and Darcy, but one should never underestimate the worth of a well-educated man in the bedroom. One can learn many things from a book (or website), and the intellectual will take them to heart . . . not to mention tongue and cock. Christopher was an architect with a background in metallurgy—which made sense, now that I thought of it, given his steel beam of a tool.

Back to the Bennets, and the hubbub surrounding the Netherfield ball . . . but given my current state of randiness my brain was turning even Austen into softcore porn as I imagined the public balling planned for the stately hall, a full-fledged orgy taking place upon the Persian rugs, quite a coming out for the pre-Victorian virgins.

With the influence of the tea and the heat in my blood (not to mention my honey-humid panties), the jetlag seemed more like a narcotic or even some psychedelic drug. I wasn't feeling tired as much as high.

I'd only had sex a few times with an altered mind—most were nothing especially memorable (due to the lackluster sex, not the above-average drugs)—but a couple of times. . . .

I glanced up—and my brown-eyed Professor was gone. I was so captivated by the Bennet girls' Netherfield balling and my own tepid recollections that I'd missed his departure and a final ogling of his finely contoured caboose.

Well shoot.

Perhaps then I could get into my book. I did read for a while but soon my tea ran out and I didn't feel like a refill. It was nearly two a.m. Surely my brain would put out the white

flag and surrender to sleep if I went to bed—
perhaps a quickie with Discreet Pete, thinking
of the Professor in lieu of fucking (i.e. fuckin')
Christopher, would work as an effective grog.
I'd considered packing one of my more indus-
trial dildos but didn't want my travels compli-
cated by some sweaty Customs agent lifting it
from my bag and leering his (or her) approval.

I started my short hike back to the Renaissance. They say New York is the city that never
sleeps but Chicago is no slouch in that department. Several couples and small groups were
returning from bars or wherever.

I'd only gone a block or so when I noticed
a solo man coming my way—a lone pedestri-
an stood out on the sidewalk. Still, I paid little
attention to him in my psychedelic, jetlagged
fog, so I was surprised when he said, "You've
already gotten bored with the Bennets."

It was the Professor.

"The book was still interesting but the
bookshop had lost its appeal." Why was I flirting . . . so shamelessly?

Even in the utilitarian lighting of
streetlamps and shop windows his smile was

perfect. "Actually I was fetching something to share with you."

I noticed the white paper bag in his hand.

"You ever had an egg sandwich from Koloski's?"

"Can't say that I have . . ."

"I went wholegrain—you seem like fitness is important. Hopefully you're not vegan . . . I mean in terms of this particular offering."

I could smell the sandwich, a bit sweet like butter. "What makes you think my husband would be all right with me sharing an egg sandwich with a strange man?"

He smiled again. A lock of hair fell over the frame of his glasses and I wanted to brush it in place with my finger. "I took a risk," he said, "although not a big one, since I didn't see a ring—wedding, promise or otherwise. So . . . can I entice you back to Ruben's with the best egg sandwich in the city?"

He was taller than I'd guessed. If he took me in his arms, my head would fit nicely beneath his chin. He waited, *œuful* offering in one hand, thick book in the other.

"No . . ." I said, "I have a better place in

mind." I started walking again toward my ho-tel—of course the Professor had no way of deducing that. Perhaps I was taking him to another little hole-in-the-wall—it seemed the Windy City was riddled with them—or to my favorite park bench, or to an alley to go down on him between bites of buttery egg sandwich.

It seemed this would be an opportune time to introduce ourselves, but apparently we both preferred anonymity. He was the Professor, and I was perhaps Lydia Bennet. I could sense his inquisitiveness, his wondering where I was leading him, his wondering if I was going to partake of sandwich then blue-ball him back into the night, or whether I'd be tonguing his balls before dawn. I was wondering too.

I could sense his growing excitement as we made our path along the sidewalk of mostly closed shops and boutiques. It seemed that we should be talking, getting to know one another, but the jetlag had shut down the word-making part of my brain, and I was operating more by instinct. I was keenly aware of the smell of the food mixed with my own moist scent of desire.

The Professor was silent too. His mind had

to be racing with the possibilities before him. Perhaps he was content to linger in his imagination and not break the spell with small talk.

Without warning or announcement I entered the revolving doors of the Renaissance into its glittering lobby. The Professor may have hesitated for a moment before following me inside. I smiled and nodded to the two women who had the honor of working overnight at the registration desk. The tall black guy in the gray suit leaning on the desk was no doubt hotel security.

I fished the keycard out of my jeans' back pocket as the Professor caught up, giving us the appearance of a couple. The elevator doors opened and we stepped inside. I slid the key card into the slot to give us access to the club member floors, and I couldn't help thinking of other things slipping into other places, tongues and cocks and fingers. I thought of knocking the silly egg sandwich from his hand and pinning him against the mirrored wall of the swiftly ascending car, and of him dropping the silly bag and pinning me against the wall—but instead the doors opened and we were on my floor.

It was a lengthy walk to my room, around a corner, and I found myself slowing on purpose, mischievously turning up the suspense. Finally, though, we reached my room, and were quickly inside.

The Professor set the sack on the credenza. "Home sweet home," he said.

I continued in a nearly hypnotic haze, except that physically I felt like a caged leopard—a strange disconnect between mind and body, and it seemed that only one thing would make me whole: a screamingly intense orgasm, something downright operatic, or perhaps a half dozen Wagnerian spasms of pleasure. I wondered if the Professor had it in him.

He was still holding his thick book: *Against the Day*, Pynchon. I'd read *Gravity's Rainbow* in grad school, wasn't a fan, but recalled some of the book's perversions, like Brigadier Pudding's coprophilial copulation with Katje. Live and let live, I say, but sucking on freshly pooped poop doesn't do it for me.

I pulled my sweater off, mussing my hair but not caring, and I know he didn't either. I was glad I'd worn my black bra with the lace and just a touch of push-up. Girls with big tits are supposed to be sexy but I've found men respond to B-cups quite enthusiastically too.

The Professor put down Pynchon and came to me.

For a moment we looked at one another. His brown eyes were flecked with gold or green, something unexpected.

I reached beneath my breasts and unhooked the bra's front closure. He took me by the shoulders and kissed me as I reached up and ran my fingers through his hair, which I'd wanted to do since I first saw him in Ruben's.

The tips of our tongues met, and I plunged my tongue into his mouth again and again, as he sucked it. He seemed well-practiced with his mouth and lips—a harbinger of good things perhaps.

His hands released my tits from their lacey cups. I let go of his head long enough for him to push the bra's little black straps off my shoulders. His hands, only slightly callused from some long-ago labor, returned to my tits and his thumbs grazed my nipples, which were as hard as candy.

I pushed against him and felt his cock pushing back inside his jeans. I released from our kiss and unbuttoned the top button of his shirt, then the next, and so on . . . I placed my hands flat against his chest, which was nicely developed and just hairy enough. I pushed off his shirt, feeling the hard muscles of shoulders and arms, and kissed and sucked one of his nipples. He approved.

We stood apart for a moment and removed our pants, everything except his pinstriped boxers (nice) and my black lace thong. I'd hit the jackpot. He was beautiful—clearly he worked in visits to the gym in addition to the library. He wasn't over musclebound, like some steroid freak, but in good shape, with a flat stomach and gorgeous legs—he ran or biked or something. Best of all, his cock pushed against his boxers, its head restrained by the waistband. I ached to take his cock into my mouth and feel it strain against the back of my throat. I was about to make it happen when he turned me around and started kissing my shoulders and neck. His hands cupped my breasts, supporting them while he gently squeezed my nipples between forefinger and thumb.

I wanted him inside me: his tongue, his cock, his fingers, in my mouth, my throat, my cunt, my ass, everywhere.

He kissed my ear, his lips soft and warm, and slid one hand down my tummy, hesitating at the low cut of my panties. I wondered if he would finger my clit (I wanted him to), but after a moment he put his hand on top of the crotch of my thong, just holding the heat of my pussy. He must've felt how little hair I allow down south, just a little brown line of fluff.

I turned my head and Frenched with his expert tongue again. His hands found the bare cheeks of my ass. A finger tugged gently on the thong, tightening it against my soaking cunt, the thin silk strap running along my taint.

I thought of Christopher and the way he'd place a fingertip in my asshole while he ate my pussy. It drove me crazy, and I hoped the Professor had a similar technique in his lesson plans. If not, I may have to school him.

In one graceful movement he picked me up. I thought he'd take me to the bed—having had his fill of foreplay (I was nicely full)—but instead he went to the large leather chair in the corner and sat with me in his lap. His patience was remarkable. I felt his cock against my thigh. He had buttons on the fly of his boxers, and I wondered that it was painful for his dong to press against the buttons, which dug into my skin just a bit. Perhaps he liked the pain a little. We kissed like long-parted lovers for a long time, increasing my desire for him. Then he leaned me back against the arm of the chair and had at my tits as if he'd desired them forever. He kissed and licked and sucked them with abandon, I thought my desire couldn't be any keener, but his mouth and tongue and teeth on my tits and nipples nearly made me come.

I couldn't take it any longer. I lifted his face from my breasts and got off his lap. He started to rise too, but I held him back. I was on my knees and he got the idea. I didn't want him to lose the boxers—or the glasses for that matter!—so I unbuttoned the fly and helped his cock out into the world.

My mouth watered at its length and girth, and it was nicely veined, with all roads leading to the purple head, where I began my kissing and licking, sucking up the dollop of pre-cum at its glistening eye.

Then I deep-throated the Professor's perfect pointer with a quick slurp, and slowly returned my lips up his shaft. The rock-hard ridges drove me wild as I imagined that nicely marbled meat plunging into my pussy. I've been with men who were as quiet as choirboys as I sucked their shafts, but I prefer men who moan their approval, and the Professor didn't disappoint in that department either. His head was back and his fingers played in my hair, keeping it out of my face as I corkscrewed my lips around his cock, again and again, then licked and sucked his head.

I was tempted to finish him, to go down on him until his hot cum erupted in my throat, but before I could decide, he stopped me himself, lifted me up and led me to the bed. He whipped back the covers, and we crawled on top of the Renaissance's silky sheets. Immediately my head was cradled in his strong arm and we were kissing, our tongues quickly cuddling, exploring each other's mouth. I felt the weight of his stiff cock, still protruding from his boxers, resting on my thigh. Meanwhile his fingers lay on the crotch of my panties, pushing gently on my pussy, driving me crazy—I needed him to eat me or fuck me, something. Kissing was fantastic but I had to have more. Now.

At last he pulled away. His lips lingered at my nipples a moment, but he sensed what I really wanted, and how much I wanted it. He skipped down my tummy, tonguing my belly-button for a second or two, tightening the tension of my desire even more.

Finally his face was between my legs. He kissed the insides of my thighs before quickly moving his mouth to my dripping pussy. He nuzzled my clit through my panties and I let out a little moan of my own. He pulled my panties tight so that they pressed against my clit, and the edges of my love-swollen lips were exposed on either side. He discovered just how hairless I keep my quim and he began licking the lips of my pussy around the edges of my thong, long, sure strokes of his tongue. I loved it.

Then he moved the wet crotch of my thong to one side and dipped his tongue deep into the juices of my pussy. I bit my lip in pleasure. His tongue darted to my clit and really went to work. I shut my eyes and bit my lip harder, accepting the pleasure he bestowed. His tongue stroked and flicked me toward climax. I gripped the sheets and put my feet on his shoulders. I'd needed this sort of pussy eating, and ate up every second.

After a time—I'd lost track of how much—he raised himself up enough to remove my panties altogether. I thought he was ready to fuck me. Instead he went back to work on my cunt. My God. His tongue was everywhere, and everyplace was perfect. He alternated between licking and kissing my clit—his face must've glistened with my honeyed juice!—and running his tongue along the rim of my pussy, up one side of my clit, then back down, like the swinging motion of a pendulum, around the rim and up the other side. I'd never had that technique before. It was exquisite and kept me on the frantic cusp of coming. The pleasure was luxurious and excruciating. I wanted to come.

I spoke the first words either of us had said since the sidewalk near Ruben's: "Take me with your tongue."

And he obliged, wildly licking and sucking my engorged clit—until I felt the wave of orgasm crashing through my body, tensing every muscle, my thighs gripping his head. As he felt me coming he reached up and pinched my nipples while he fucked me with his tongue, each thrust nipping the crest of my clit, amplifying my orgasm. Jesus, I thought or said or screamed. Who knows.

Maybe it wasn't a word at all, just a loud animal release of carnal pleasure.

I put my fingers in his hair. He knew when my coming was through and came up for air. He held me while I wrapped myself around his leanly muscled body, smelling my sex all over him. I was lightheaded and had only one thought in my muddled mind: his delicious dong. He had gone down on me for so long his tool had lost a touch of intensity, but I knew how to e-rectify that. I pushed him on his back and went down on him. In no time he was fully hard against my lips and tongue.

I sat up and helped him out of his boxers, then straddled him and slipped his gorgeous dick inside me. He filled me to the brim and the sensation of mounting him nearly made me come again.

I began fucking him slowly. I realized he still had on his glasses, and even that was a turn-on. After a few thrusts he held my hips and said, "Turn around." I happily repositioned myself reverse cowgirl—again his granite-veined cock sliding in its full length nearly made me orgasm.

I reached between his thighs and gently squeezed his egg-sized balls. I let the tip of my middle finger graze his butthole.

He steadied my hips. "Lie back," he said. "Stretch out."

I did as told. His cock still rested firmly and fully in my cunt. I reclined so that my back was on his chest, and I stretched out my legs so all my weight was resting on him. The angle of his cock pressing against my g-spot filled my whole cunt with pleasure.

He swept aside my hair and began kissing and nibbling my neck and ear while he caressed my breasts.

His breath was hot in my ear, reminding me of its heat on my clit only moments before. "Squeeze me with your pussy," he said.

I began using the muscles of my cunt to hug his dick, in lieu of fucking him. I had felt pleasure—now that pleasure was pulsating. I couldn't stop myself and came again with a moan as his tongue tunneled into my ear.

"Keep going," he whispered, fingering my nipples.

He was indeed a well-educated man. He'd formed our bodies into a kind of orgasm-making machine. With every squeeze or two of his cock another cascade of coming rippled through my body. I braced myself with my hands on his hips. I felt higher and more light-headed than I'd ever been. The world was his mouth at my neck and the corpus of steady pleasure between my legs, and all my cunt had to do was tighten to unleash another sonic orgasm.

I lost count. I was incapable of speech let alone numbers. I came again and again, moaning, screaming until I felt myself growing hoarse. It's a wonder security didn't pound on the door.

My body went slack from exhaustion. He gave me a moment or two, then he began rocking my hips with his hands. I helped as much as I could with my trembling legs. A minute, five minutes, more orgasms . . . and finally the Professor came. He pushed my cunt as far as it could go and his cock quaked inside of me. I imagined him filling me with a quart of cum as he moaned his own pleasure in my ear.

I wouldn't have thought it possible but I came a final time as the last of his spunk spurted into the darkest region of my quivering cunt.

I was through. I rolled off him and fell asleep as if anesthetized.

I woke to bright daylight streaming through my parted curtains. I had the sense that it was late morning, but when I read the clock on the nightstand it said 2:12. Holy crap, I'd slept for nearly ten hours. I recalled the orgasmathon. As cliché as it sounds, it had all the aspects of a dream, except that as I moved in bed my body confirmed the intensity of the lovemaking. My thighs and abs and even my vaginal muscles were sore. I reached between my legs and traced where he'd spun my golden orgasms, too numerous to count.

I sensed I was alone in the room. I sat up in the large bed and confirmed he was gone. The bathroom's frosted-glass door was pushed aside on its track and the light was off. I recalled the shower's pulsating jets and nothing sounded so good in the world. I was famished but a hot shower was number-one on the list.

As I scooted myself out of bed, I discovered even more sore muscles. After college I'd gotten into triathlons for a while. The morning-after feeling was similar to this, including the residual bliss from the flood of endorphins.

I looked around for my phone and it was charging on the nightstand opposite the one with the clock. I didn't remember plugging it in. Then I saw beneath it a handwritten note on the hotel's pad of paper: *Didn't want to wake you. Tonight, 7 p.m. Newberry Library – Thank you!?*

My jeans and sweater were neatly folded

over the back of the chair next to the desk, and my bra on top of them. What a gentleman. Still no name, nor even a cell number, but this invitation for a second *date*, so to speak.

The fuck had been perfect—why risk tarnishing a perfect thing? I slid the note from beneath my phone and deposited it in the waste basket on my way to the bathroom.

I had twenty-four hours before meeting the Kims, and I still needed the 3 Rs: reading, resting and researching. A lot of what my clients paid me for was my knowledge of the area I was guiding them through, and one can never be too well-informed.

My day was uneventful. In the afternoon I managed a token effort in the fitness center (too sore from the fuck to do much). Nevertheless I rewarded myself with some window shopping on Michigan Avenue. Nothing much caught my eye. Besides, when I left Paris I packed for Singapore, and not this junket to Chicago, so my bags were already adequately full. Thanks to thousands of hours of practice, I was an expert traveler, specializing in not over-packing. You could purchase almost anything you needed or wanted anywhere in the world if you had enough money and knew where to shop or whom to contact.

The unhurried unraveling of my day was relaxing but thoughts of the Professor and his note kept intruding. It sounded a bit like he was inviting me out—sort of reverse engineering a relationship, starting with the unbridled sex, then moving toward the awkward first date conversation over cocktails. No thanks.

I'd be meeting the Doctors Kim in about eighteen hours. The last thing I needed was a first date. Now, if the fantastic fuck was followed by an even more fantastic fuck . . . but why risk it?

I stopped in the hotel's bar for a glass of chardonnay while catching up on some emails via my phone and the Renaissance's wi-fi. I figured, a little more reading in my room, then maybe some room service and a movie with a little more chardonnay—and I'd be ready for bed. My internal clock was adjusting but I was still feeling a trifle sluggish. I'd be getting fully in sync just about the time I'd be beginning my day-long flight to Singapore. It's an occupational hazard.

There were a couple of suits at the bar checking me out, young, fresh-out-of-the-wrapper attorneys or financial guys, good-looking—one, the blonde, was especially cute. But I was in no mood for chitchat, and, besides, younger men were enthusiastic (which has its merits) but were usually unpracticed and too likely to fall in love after Frenching, let alone fucking.

I looked up from my phone to catch the cute one in the act. I smiled, a little, but that was all he'd be getting, from me anyway. Maybe he could find some horny college girl later who'd do the nude watusi on his wand. More likely he'd be transporting his blue balls back to his shitty apartment and jerking off to some Internet porn.

The image of the Professor's nicely veined prick came to me and I felt a tingle in my clit—

No more of that! I returned my attention to the emails and chardonnay. Before long I was headed to the elevator, leaving behind the leering suits and their ten-dollar drinks.

IN MY ROOM, I kicked off my shoes and

glanced through the room-service menu, though I wasn't ready to order yet. Then I clicked through the movie choices. I had no intention of sitting alone in my room watching porn, but I was curious about the adult entertainment options:

Sorority Steam Room—The Alpha Angels raise money for charity by raising the sauna temperature to super hot!

Field of MILFs—A pride of cougars helps the local college team get up for the big game!

Dr. Deborah: Sexologist—Couples needing some creativity in the bedroom seek the doctor's hands-on advice.

A-Plus for Effort!—College co-eds require tutoring from the new TA, who's ripped, well-studied, and prefers group sessions!

All right . . . I clicked off the TV. That last one hit too close to home. The maid had emptied the waste baskets, but I recalled the location the Professor had written on the notepad. I called the concierge: I'd need a cab in ten minutes—enough time to touch up my make-up, gather my hair into a ponytail, and grab my go-to sandals and jean jacket.

I had second thoughts while riding in the taxi, but the cabbie's reckless romp through the city left me little time to fret. We were quickly in front of the Newberry Library. I swiped my card, punched in a $5 tip, grabbed my purse and was on the sidewalk. It was five to seven. There was a potential *ménage à trois* (two chicks and a dude) going up the steps, so I turned it into a three-on-one and followed them in. They seemed to know where they were going. We went down a noisy tiled hall to a room called the Towner Fellows' Lounge. It was set up with chairs and couches, and a baby grand piano in the corner. The event was nicely attended, maybe forty people, but there were seats open here and there. I picked one toward the back and had to excuse myself past a couple of foreign-looking guys, Middle Eastern or Italian maybe—either way, I think they were o.k. with my tightly bluejeaned tush being in their faces for a second or two.

The Lounge was elegant with tall bookcases built into the paneled walls, and a rich crimson carpet. A wide range of ages were in attendance, but younger on average, including some college kids—maybe more females than males.

I was trying to spot my fuck buddy without being too obvious . . . then there was a woman at the podium in the front of the room—forty-ish, blond (not natural but a quality dye job), good makeup, o.k. shape, not bad boobs, plum dress. She was doing the introductions for the speaker, Thomas Kincaid, whom she referred to as Tom after the initial reference. And there he was in the front row, back to me, but I recognized the hair spilling over the collar of his sport coat. With his head angled toward the blonde, I could see the black-framed glasses too. *Tom*. I liked *Thomas* better. She was going on and on about "Tom" and his books, how fabulous they were. She was sleeping with him, I could tell. This lavish intro amounted to giving him head in public. I was all right with it. Good for him, dipping his dick into his cougar colleague from time to time.

Finally she took his prick out of her mouth and brought Thomas Kincaid to the podium. He looked darn good. Blue jeans, white shirt open at the collar a button more than necessary, black sport coat. He thanked the cougar,

Zoe somebody, for the generous public knob-job.

He had a book in hand, *his* book, a collection of novellas, *Pastels for Allende*. He was going to read an excerpt from the title novella. He had a good speaking voice, manly without being too deep, nicely paced. He was at ease in front of the group.

His writing was interesting—I'd have to download his books to my Fire—but I was having trouble concentrating: this bizarre fantasy was materializing in my brain, which was maybe still a little jetlagged. To back track, I'd gone to a couple of live sex shows, years before, and discovered they really weren't my *thang*. Yet I began thinking of something like that. I get up from my chair and walk to the front of the room. Looking at the audience I remove every stitch of clothing—not vampishly, rather, businesslike. I finish with my black lace thong, which I step out of, kicking aside with my toe. I let everyone get a good look, especially Zoe the cougar, before turning to start undressing Thomas Kincaid, author and orgasm machine. He continues reading to the audience while I slide off his jacket, unbutton his shirt and jeans, and pull down the zipper. He isn't annoyed, but determined to keep reading *Pastels for Allende*. He has to cooperate for me to disrobe him, switching his book from hand to hand, for instance, when I remove his jacket and shirt.

When we are as nude as Adam and Eve, I slip between his arms and begin kissing his neck and chest. The audience is transfixed by the spectacle, and Thomas Kincaid's mesmerizing plot. I kiss and suck and finger his nipples as he goes on reading. His cock has long since come to attention, so I drop to my knees and begin licking and sucking, sucking and licking, kissing. It requires great concentration but he doesn't miss a word while I deep throat him to complete concrete dong status. I'm somewhat obscured by the podium, though it's a narrow one; however, the people in the first few rows have a clear enough view of the back of my head bobbing on the authorial cock. The sound of my sucking is loud in the stately room, punctuating Thomas Kincaid's literary masterpiece.

The fragrance of my dripping cunt fills the room, making everyone horny as hell, yet they hang on his every word. I stop fellating him, stand and face the audience. My lips are glossy with saliva and pre-cum. Everyone is pin-drop quiet and wide-eyed. I take hold of the podium and push the author back with my ass. When I'm just the right distance I spread my feet. Book in one hand and dick in the other, he guides his missile into my juicy cunt. At first he fucks me slowly while he continues to read his novella. I purr every time he glides his tool past my parted lips, deeper, deeper, deeper into my eager pussy, then out, out, out again, and again.

The novella's plot begins picking up in intensity—something about a young girl lost in a darkening jungle—and even the coolheaded Thomas Kincaid has trouble maintaining his concentration. He pauses long enough to hand me the book and point out where he'd stopped. I then begin reading to the audience about the girl in the jungle, while the author places his hands on my hips and starts fucking me hard. His cock cruises into my cunt, and I feel his rollicking balls slap at my clit in his furious fucking.

My voice is unsteady as we get closer and closer to coming. I'm in mid-sentence when I feel his rocketing orgasm, which catapults me over the edge too, and I moan an ecstatic exclamation point, dropping my face into the open pages of his book, my pleasure is so complete. My orgasm is still glowing in my pussy when I toss the book to Zoe the cougar in the front row and I quickly turn and go down on Thomas Kincaid to gobble every last drop from the dripping tip of his glistening cock. . . .

It didn't quite happen that way, except for the story about the girl in the jungle and my increasing appetite for his dick. He was a good reader and often looked up from his text. At one point he spied me in the audience. It took him a moment to recognize me with my hair back and glasses. It was the only time he slipped a bit in his reading, doing something of a verbal double take at seeing me. I was pleased. Zoe the cougar noticed his minor flub and looked over her shoulder to find little ol' me. She was good: her bitches-and-hos radar was finely tuned. We talk about rappers and their misogynistic and sexist lyrics—but there is no one more brutal to a woman than another woman who feels her sex territory is being poached by an invading cunt. I know; I've been there.

Zoe's eyes iced over and she turned back toward the Professor, who'd regained his composure—although his pacing was perhaps a bit quicker, to match his quickening pulse, or his stiffening dick. I settled in and began enjoying the reading even more. Who gave a flying fuck about the girl in the jungle? It was enthralling to watch Thomas Kincaid when he knew I was in the audience. Maybe my Wagnerian, orgiastic shrieks of yester-evening echoed still in his ears as he tried to concentrate on his narrative.

He concluded after about twenty minutes, leaving us with a cliffhanger: the girl is cornered in a clearing with a black leopard closing in. I suppose some may read the leopard as symbolic of evil in the world, poised to destroy Innocence—sort of how the white whale represents evil in *Moby Dick*. But speaking of dick, I saw Thomas Kincaid's story differently. The leopard is "long" and "sleek" and "powerful"—so, come on, the leopard is a penis, and a big black one at that. It's slowly approaching (foreplay) the innocent girl (virgin). In fact, as the scene closes she's about to be eaten. I'm no Northrop Frye, but the symbolism ain't that tricky. No doubt I was helped along by thinking of the Professor's inspired munching of my cunt. In particular I was recalling that pendulum technique with his tongue around the rim of my pussy. I'd buy a ticket for that ride again.

I fidgeted in my chair, horny heat building between my thighs.

The Professor invited questions from the audience. There were two or three mundane ones about his inspiration and his process, yadda yadda. His responses were mildly interesting—more so than the questions deserved—and he had an easy manner with the audience, and those nice teeth.

I couldn't help myself; I had to spice things up. "Does your story promote violence toward women?" I hadn't even raised my hand. "Or do you see the young girl's being eaten as a kind of homage to her?"

A big dose of those nice teeth. "Well, first off, it's not clear what's going to happen with her. Will she be eaten or not? That's still up in the air." Zoe the cougar was glaring back at me, as if she wanted to eat me, but not in a good way. The Professor continued, "As far as violence toward women, I certainly hope not. I'm rather fond of them."

There were a couple of college girls directly in front of me, probably worshipful students of Professor Kincaid's, and I think they came right then and there.

"I'm intrigued," I said. "Will she be eaten or not? Does the leopard have something else in mind? Does *she*?"

The Professor just responded with those brown eyes and that smile.

Zoe popped up. "Thank you, Tom, and thank you everyone for coming . . ." She paused a beat. ". . . Tom will be at the table in back signing books. Please, have some wine and hors d'oeuvres"—she said *hors d'oeuvres* as French as possible, nearly spraining her tongue—"and pick up a copy of *Pastels for Allende*. It's marvelous, as you have heard."

What the hell; in for a penny, in for a pound. I got myself a glass of chardonnay (mediocre), bought a copy of the Professor's book, and took my place in line to have him sign it. The college girls were ahead of me still, which slowed things down—they were so enthusiastic and thorough in their praise, practically getting themselves off in the process. One of them, a strawberry blonde, gushed about the Professor's masterful technique. She had no idea. Or did she?

It was finally my turn at the oracle. "Nice reading," I said, handing over the book.

"I'm glad you made it. Wasn't sure you would."

"What can I say? You piqued my curiosity."

He opened the book to the title page. "And to whom may I inscribe it?"

I hesitated, to let the suspense build. "To Esmée—spelled the French way . . ."

Without hesitating he began

To Esmée –

I was impressed. In the States I normally had to spell my name for people, and I rarely bothered with the diacritical mark, as it could end up on any of the *e*'s, once or twice even the *s* and *m* were mistakenly adorned. (When Christopher and I first met, we noted the deceptive nature of our names—he was a French-man with an English name, and I an American with a French one.) Thomas Kincaid paused to think what to write. After a second or two his pen began skipping across the page. I may have been able to read it upside-down, but I resisted.

He handed me the book. "Staying long? At the reception I mean."

I looked around. We were holding up the line. "Probably not. I leave for Singapore to-morrow. I'd like to go to bed."

"Sleepy?"

"Not in the least. Thanks for signing my book." I smiled, picked up a complimentary bookmark from the table and walked away. I Ubered a ride and finished my wine. By the time I went outside the car was there.

Back in my room, I didn't know if the Professor would pay me a visit—maybe the cougar would entice him to a helping of tried-and-true pussy—but I figured he'd be calling. I thought about ordering a bottle of wine, but that seemed too much like a date, like the beginning of a relationship. I really just wanted another stellar fuck then to board my flight to

Singapore. I had no plans to be in Chicago in the foreseeable future, which was just as well.

Music seemed a good idea, not so much to set the mood but to mask the operatic orgasms. There was a docking station by the bed, so I connected to Spotify and went to my "Jazz" folder. Wynton Marsalis flowed through the speakers. I turned up the volume a click. I wondered if the Professor had other tricks up his sleeve. Even if he was only a one-trick pony, I'd gladly have another performance before leaving town.

I changed into a pair of cotton running shorts that were so skimpy no girl would try running in them. They should just market them as cotton cock-teasers. That's what they were. Before the running shorts, I also traded my thong for a black v-string, the tiniest panties I owned. The thong I took off were Granny bloomers by comparison. I added a clingy white sleeveless t-shirt (o.k., a "wife-beater"), with no bra. The only way to broadcast my intentions more plainly would've been to have READY TO BE FUCKED in neon-pink letters across my tits.

In all my sex prep I'd forgotten about Thomas Kincaid's inscription in the book. I picked up *Pastels for Allende* from the desk and plopped in a chair. He'd written,

To Esmée –

Your hospitality is unsurpassed. Ruben's has always been a special place, but now . . .

Well, it wasn't Sonnet #18, no comparison to a summer's day, or any other season's, which was all right. But the inscription was honest and mysterious enough to make people wonder, when the book is eventually passed on to other hands.

I assumed the Professor would call, but stranger things have happened. While I read the book I also lightly revisited the times I'd been stood up or dumped unceremoniously. (What would a dumping ceremony entail? Probably *unceremoniously* was better.)

I was getting chilly, with so much bare skin, so I turned back the bed covers, and slid under them with my book. I thought I might like to act out my fantasy from the reading, improvise the back of the desk chair for the podium maybe. But, no, it wouldn't be close to the same thing without the element of exhibition, of fucking in front of the select crowd of brainiacs—and especially of fucking before the jealous gaze of Zoe the cougar. . . .

Wait, what if he brings her along, in the mood for a threesome? I'd only been a party to such an arrangement, appropriately, thrice. One time with two men, in Rio, twin brothers actually, sons of a diplomat from Paraguay, something like that. It was all right; they were handsome and attentive. The other two times with a man and another chick. Neither experience did much for me. The guys seemed more interested in watching us chicks do each other. Generally speaking I'm not into women. So it was unlikely that I'd find a three-way with Thomas Kincaid and Zoe to my taste. But never say never.

The hotel phone by the bed rang.

"Hi, it's Tom. I'm downstairs. Would you like to come down for a drink, or we could grab a bite somewhere?"

How adorable. "No thanks. Why don't you just come up? I'll call the desk to punch you up." He seemed o.k. with that arrangement.

Also, no mention of the cougar.

I called the desk, then got up and checked myself in the mirror. It seemed to take longer than it should. Eventually though a tap-tap-tapping on my door.

He came in, bottle of wine in hand, a merlot. Again, adorable, that he felt compelled to pretend this wasn't just a hook-up, this wasn't just about us fucking like pros.

"Thanks." I sat the wine on the desk.

"Would you like some?" he asked.

"Not at the moment—"

He took me into his arms and kissed me, tipping back my head and our tongues instantly began their dance. He picked me up by holding my ass and I wrapped my legs around his hips as he carried me the few steps to the big chair. He sat. My legs were still wrapped around him. He kissed my face, my neck, my lips again, his hands were under my shirt massaging my back, cupping my breasts. I thought he might take off the wife-beater, but he seemed to like it on, for now anyway. He nibbled at my nipples through the sheer material.

I braced myself against his shoulders, and

with some wiggling I managed to stand, with my feet on the arms of the chair and one knee against its back. It was a little awkward but it brought me closer to his face. He caught on immediately and pulled aside the crotch of my shorts and panties, and began tonguing my pussy—long, smooth laps along my clit. He put his hand beneath my shorts and held my firm ass.

I put my hand in his hair: "Yes, lick my cunt, lick it . . ." The pleasure ran through my body like a charge. He was already working me toward climax.

I stopped him and stepped down to the floor. I invited him to stand; then we proceeded to undress him, down to his undies, tighter tonight than the boxers, navy blue. His hard cock bulged and I petted it through the shorts, rubbing its tip with my thumb. I longed for its head in the back of my throat.

He guided me to the edge of the bed, and he knelt before me, apparently wanting more pussy—who was I to deny him? He peeled off the little running shorts, which left the microscopic black panties. He rubbed my clit and lips with his thumb while he kissed and licked the insides of my thighs, driving me crazy.

He nuzzled and kissed my sex, his mouth grazing the lips of my cunt on either side of the panties' narrow crotch. I was bathed in pleasure. I wanted his tongue to fuck me, to do that pendulum thing with the rim of my cunt. I. Wanted. It.

Instead, he kissed his way north and licked my bellybutton. It was nice, and a line ran down to my pussy, making it tingle and throb with desire.

"Lie on your stomach," he said while kissing around my navel.

He helped me out of the wife-beater as I moved to the middle of the bed and lay flat, wondering what the Professor had in mind. He crawled on his hands and knees until he was above me. He began kissing my ear, my neck, and quickly moved to my shoulders. His warm lips and the tip of his tongue moved across my shoulder blades, my spine. His hands were on my shoulders, my ribs. He got me hotter and hotter—his patience was a turn-on itself . . . as was his rock-cock bumping along my butt and thighs as he moved above me.

He reached the small of my back, kissing, licking. Then beyond the thin border of my thong. He kissed and fondled the cheeks of my ass. "A work of art," he said. His tongue moved closer and closer to the artwork's curved crack. His finger followed the trail of the thong. I lay with my hands beneath my face, eyes closed, enjoying every second of his exploration.

He moved the thong aside and I knew for certain what he desired. I raised my ass just a little, and his probing tongue found its target; warm and wet, its tip tickled my butthole. He penetrated me with his tongue while his hands went beneath my pubis and he began rubbing my clit.

Surrounded by pleasure, by both having and wanting, I lost time as his tongue slipped in and out of my most intimate orifice. After a while he stopped and whispered, "You don't have a vibrator, by chance?"

The question took me by surprise. "Actually . . ." I moved off the bed and retrieved Discreet Pete from my bag.

The Professor repositioned me, on my knees

on the edge of the bed so that he could kneel on the floor. He took off my thong, spread my cheeks, and again tongued my arse. I supported myself with one hand, switched on Pete and placed his vibrating tip against my clit, at my favorite angle.

Holy fucking Christ. The Professor enthusiastically tossing my salad and Pete working his magic on my hooded clit . . . I moaned my pleasure and held back as long as I could before giving into the shattering orgasm. My eyes were closed as it crashed its way through my body, the epicenter deep inside my dripping cave of a cunt. *Holy. Fucking. Christ.* I may have shouted it.

I shut off Pete and put him aside. I brought the Professor into bed and had him lie on his back. It was a wonder his cock hadn't ripped through his underwear, Incredible Hulk style. I kissed his stomach, then flicked the tip of his head with my tongue while rubbing his dick—I could feel the veins through the stretched fabric. . . .

I released his dick by pulling off his shorts, and it bobbed in the air. I couldn't wait another second and took him in my mouth. I deep-throated him once, then I went to work on his beautiful balls, kissing them and sucking them into my mouth, where I rolled them on my tongue. Meanwhile I continued stroking his cock, slowly, not wanting him to come anytime soon. He loved the teabag treatment and moaned his approval. His moaning nearly made me come again.

I returned to his cock in earnest, licking and kissing up and down its length, sucking its lavender head, gently squeezing his worked-over sack. At the moment, I didn't know if I could ever get enough of his cock.

"I want more of your pussy." We were kindred spirits. "Kneel above me." This one was a woman-pleaser.

I sucked him a bit longer before complying. I positioned myself above his eager mouth, gripping the upholstered headboard. He reached around my thighs to open my lips with his fingers. Then he began eating my pussy with gusto, his tongue rimming just inside my cunt before stroking my clit, rimming and stroking, stroking, rimming, stroking. He must've had a Ph.D. in cunnilingus.

I moved my hips in sync with his tongue, pushed down a trifle to get the perfect degree of pressure . . . holy mother of god . . .

White-knuckling the headboard, I put my head back as I came—his tongue fucking me and his lips hot on my pussy, amplifying the big-O. My thighs shook against the sides of his head.

I curled next to him. I wanted him to hold me while the orgasm was still lingering in my body. We kissed, and I was strong on his breath.

I only needed a minute or two before I was ready for more. I mounted him and guided him inside me. My intention was to ride him hard until he came. Our fingers interlocked and I did fuck him hard. With each downward thrust his dick blossomed pleasure throughout my body, like an unfolding flower. I was on the brink of coming again when he released my hands and held my hips.

"Wait," he said, moving me off of him. He climbed out of bed and led me by the hand to the large window overlooking the lights of Chicago, twenty-two floors below. He got behind me and kissed my neck. I felt his dick bobbing between my legs. I put my hands against the cool glass and nudged him back with my ass.

Then, standing, he pushed his cock into my pussy. I pressed against the glass and watched our reflection overlaid with the city lights and lines of cars as he fucked me for all he was worth, and in the bedroom he was a billionaire.

His flawless dick pounded my pussy, stroking my g-spot, building another climax. He reached with one hand and felt my right breast, pinching the nipple in a way that would be painful under normal circumstances—but with my quim escalating to another explosion, the pain was perfect. "Harder . . ." I moaned. Not sure what I meant, he did both, fucked me even more fiercely and pinched my nipple. I announced my coming with a scream against the glass, fogging scenic Chicago.

He must be close too.

I pulled away from him. "Sit," I said. "The desk chair."

He went and pulled it clear of the desk and did as commanded. I fell to my knees, determined to give him a blowjob he'd never forget, something to put the cougar to shame. I sucked and stroked his cock, corkscrewing its shaft with my lips, licking and kissing around the head, running my teeth and tongue across its eye. More sucking, deep, the head literally down my throat. He held the arms of the chair and groaned.

When I sensed he was on the edge, I slowed down and gave baby kisses to his head. I squeezed his ready-to-rocket cock in my hand.

"*Now*, baby . . . suck me off . . ."

One more baby kiss, then I obliged, my lips moved up and down the ridges of his delicious dick—and I felt his convulsive coming. I sucked and swallowed, sucked and swallowed . . . milking his balls with my fingers. I sucked and swallowed until I had every drop.

He raised me up. "You're amazing," he kissed in my ear.

"Couldn't've said it better myself." At that moment I thought of Christopher . . . fucking Christopher. Let Giselle have him as much as she wants, the slut. They deserve each other.

The Professor and I took turns in the bathroom. While he was showering, I ordered room service. I hadn't eaten, so to speak, and was starving. I suspected Thomas Kincaid had worked up an appetite too.

He could eat, drink some merlot, spend the night if he liked—or not. I was all right with either. We'd say our good-byes soon enough, and tomorrow I'd be on my way to Singapore with the Kims.

The world as it should be, and a beautiful memory made in the City of Broad Shoulders.

E. S. Holland holds degrees in psychology, kinesiology, and comparative literature. She has been an au pair, a university research assistant, and a personal yoga instructor. Since 2012 she has worked in the exotic travel industry. The daughter of parents with careers in foreign service, she has lived all over the world and calls no place in particular home. Under a different name, she has published poetry, travel writing, and translations in small journals, mainly in Europe. *City of Broad Shoulders* is her first book.

Photo by John Peri